Dear Giavanna,

Hi! My name is Carlo, I am the reindeer dog and I live at the North Pole with my parents Santa and Mrs. Claus. When Santa and I come to see you Christmas Eve, please leave treats out for me and Santa too! Love
Carlo

THE REINDEER
DOG

THE REINDEER DOG

Donna Marie Ferro

Library of Congress Control Number: 2017907682
ISBN: Hardcover   978-1-5434-2369-3
                 Softcover   978-1-5434-2368-6
                 eBook   978-1-5434-2367-9

Print information available on the last page.

Rev. date: 05/12/2017

To order additional copies of this book, contact:
Xlibris
1-888-795-4274
www.Xlibris.com
Orders@Xlibris.com
757278

CONTENTS

For all Children, big and small,
who believe in Santa Claus

Chapter 1

Christmas Eve

Once again, Christmas Eve had arrived and Santa Claus was ROCKING and a ROLLING in his super magical sleigh. Rudolph took the lead with his eight reindeer pals prancing and pulling the sleigh into the starry wintery night. Santa Claus was at the reins and piled high to the sky were sacks of presents and toys to be delivered all over the world. The tiny sleigh streaked like a rocket past their friend the Man in the Moon. Santa waved and jingled the sleigh bells to say hello to Mr. Moon. Its moonbeams burst into a rainbow of bright colors, lighting up the night to help them on their journey.

Santa finished bringing gifts to the hamlets of the Swiss Alps, then onto the French Riviera at a leisurely cruising speed along the coastal route from Cannes, then Nice to Monaco and across the border into Northern Italy. Jingling the reins three times, it was Santa's cue to the reindeer to make a right and then the sleigh turned away from the Mediterranean Sea. Smooth sleighing along the way as the moon shone brightly and the breeze was crisp but not frigidly cold like it was in Norway or Finland.

Rudolph made sure there was enough light beaming to see the tree tops and steep, zig-zag hills ahead of them. They glided up and up into the little villages that dotted the winding roads, going higher and higher into the hills. Santa dropped off gifts at the village homes in Pero, Casanova, and then Campomarzio, crossing over to the Five Stelle. Called the villages of the stars, they are located one after another: Stella San Bernardo, Stella Giovanni, Stella Martino, Stella Giustina, and Stella Gameragna.

The sleigh then continued on its way farther up into the hills, softly landing on the rooftop of a home in the teeny-weeny village named Alpicella, pronounced Alpeechella. Santa knew this place like the back of his hand. There were a cluster of homes scattered around the little piazza. The remaining homes were nestled amongst the terraced vineyards and gentle rolling countryside. There was one small church which overlooked the valley and the Mediterranean Sea, a mini grocery store, a restaurant, a café, and a bakery. Santa's favorite shop was the bakery where he could smell the aroma of freshly baked home-made bread. The smell of it always made him hungry, and he reminded himself to get the recipe for Mrs. Claus.

Santa thought the little place called Alpicella, which is in the Liguria Region, was a wonderful quaint little village nestled near the Italian Alps. He remembered the ancient history of the Ligures Tribe, from which this region got its namesake, Liguria. They were a fierce tribe of warriors who spanned their victories across most of Europe at least two thousand years before Christ was born. After many battles they became part of the Roman Empire. Eventually a small area of Italy near the French border facing the Mediterranean Sea, called the "mezza luna," the half-moon, was all that remained of the ancient Ligures Tribe.

Santa Claus recalled how the region of Liguria and the many little villages, such as Alpicella, still have that same resilient quality of strength as their ancestors. They are strongly bonded to one another, their families and their rugged land. They turn their backs to the sea and hold their families tightly from all those who have tried to invade them for hundreds of years. This is the land of the proud people of Liguria and the little village called Alpicella.

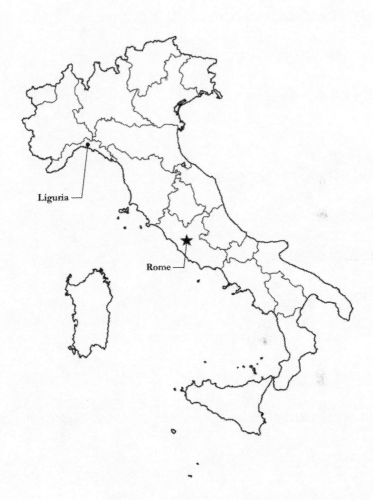

Map of Italy Showing the Region of Liguria

Chapter 2

The Goofy Witches of Beigua

Santa looked around the village. He thought something was wrong because it was freezing cold and the ground was covered with huge mounds of snow. It had never been like this when he and the reindeer visited on Christmas Eve. In all of the hundreds of years of coming here it had snowed only two or three times, and that was just a light dusting of snow that made the village look like a Christmas postcard. Santa looked down from the rooftop and spied a huge snowball over by a tree. It looked like the bottom half of a snowman. How can there be this much snow, he wondered. "Oh! No," he said out loud. "It is those darn witches, the witches of Beigua," pronounced Behgwa. Beigua is a deeply forested area above Alpicella where the goofy witches lived.

7

Goofy you may ask? Santa had met a few of them as he delivered presents up in Beigua. One time one of the goofy witches named Florinda was frolicking and flying alongside Santa's sleigh upside down on her broom with her dog Alessandro and nearly collided with the sleigh! Santa had to land in the forested area of Beigua to check his sleigh for damages. While inspecting his sleigh, he heard the goofy witches cackling, singing and dancing with their brooms while they were trying to cast spells and make potions. When he peeked at their book of spells he realized they had scribbled it in a mumbo jumbo language that made no sense! They definitely had some screws loose in their tiny pinheads.

Speaking of pinheads, the hats worn by the Beguia Witches were not the typical fashion worn by most witches. Their hats look something like a Peter Pan hat in green wool, and on the side is a long pointed black feather, with three small feathers of green, white and red representing the Italian Flag. Quite a fashion statement for witches, but then again these were not your ordinary witches found in most places, these were the Italian witches of Beigua! They selected this unusual hat by accident! When the witches came to Beigua they saw the Italian military hats of a very elite group called the Alpini, the Alpine. The Alpini are the oldest active mountain infantry in the world. This military group protected the mountainous borders of Italy from other invaders.

The witches liked the hats so much that they decided to copy them! Yes, feathers and all! And they felt their duty was also to protect the borders and the little villages such as Alpicella. The truth is the people of Alpicella found the Beigua Witches to be more of a pest, like mosquitoes swarming on a hot summer's night, rather than guardians of their homes.

The leader of the Beigua Witches, Luce Lampa, was continuously trying to do magical things but they ended up going wacky wrong! For instance, one time she turned her sidekick, Esmeralda, into an alligator by accident when she was trying to make a potion to remove wrinkles! Esmeralda also really messes up the concoctions, like the time in July when it was supposed to be a sunny afternoon for a huge outdoor party in the village. All of the town's folks and people from other villages came to the party in Alpicella. Esmeralda thought she would turn up the heat, but instead her spell made it rain as if it was winter and everyone went home drenched.

"Hmm," thought Santa, "I bet one of those goofy witches tried to cast a spell this evening so it would lightly snow like powdered sugar on top of frosted cookies. But instead they got their potions and spells mixed up, and now the tiny village is almost completely buried under the heavy blanket of snow. Well, I am too busy right now to help them and I better get going. There are a lot more presents to deliver and now is not the time to chat with those goofy witches of Beigua."

Santa made a mental note. He thought that perhaps when he returned home and had more time, he would send Luce Lampa a message about correcting their misguided spells and potions. He thought it would be best if he spelled and translated each word of their mumbo jumbo language so they could understand the correct formulas for spells, potions and other concoctions. Yes, Santa knew all the languages of the world, even the goofy mumbo jumbo language of the Beigua Witches. They certainly were not like any other witch group he had ever known, and Santa found them to be quite scatter-brained and loony. But he had a soft spot in his heart for these funny little creatures with their pointed heads! They meant no harm and all they wanted to do was to have fun!

Chapter 3

My Stars, What is it!

Santa went back to work, pulling sacks full of goodies off the sleigh, when he heard a STRANGE sound coming from under the snowy ground. Santa has many super magical powers and one them is his extraordinary hearing. He can move his ears in and out and up and down! Did you know he can even hear a butterfly hiccup from miles and miles away? Santa quickly turned to Rudolph and said, "Hey Rudy, turn on your highest nose beam, I hear something over there by that tree with the huge snowball!" Rudolph BOOSTED his nose so bright it BEAMED like the North Star.

The icy cold North wind was WAILING like a band of BANSHEES. It was as if they were practicing one of their songs they would sing at night while flying among the pine trees and mountainsides. Santa knew there were some not so very nice folks called Banshees lurking way up above the village in the deep, dark forest. The Banshees are usually found in Ireland, but centuries ago a group pledged to fight alongside the Ligures Tribe and eventually ended up above Beguia near the tippy top of the mountainside. They were much more clever than the goofy merry mischief makers, Beigua witches.

During the summer months, the poor folks of Alpicella often suffered from a lack of sleep. Many nights just before dawn they would wake up to the thunderous racket from the Banshees and Beigua Witches. They would listen to their shrilling voices, cackling and screaming at one another as they played the Italian game of Bocce Ball. This sport is like the ancient Roman's version of bowling only it is played outside. Sometimes, the witches and their faithful dogs, cats and barnyard friends, such as goats, chickens, and pigs, zoomed along on their broomsticks at supersonic speed and crashed into the villagers' windows as they were gleefully cheering on the Beigua Witches' Team! The Beigua Witches were not the best at broom driving. Thank heavens they did not drive a car! The final score in every game was the same, Banshees Ten and Beigua Witches, Zip! ZERO! The Beigua witches always plotted against the Banshees in hopes that one day they would win. So far they have been the Champs of Losing!

Santa turned his attention back to the snowball by the tree, and with his extraordinary hearing he cocked his head towards the ground, and then it happened! He heard a whimpering sound and it was growing louder and louder, then he saw the snowball moving, it was rocking back and forth. It was like something was trying to get out! Santa turned to Rudy and said, "I think there is something inside that huge snowball!" Rudolph pushed the power to SUPER spotlight mode. Of course Rudolph has a magical nose… well, you know the rest of that story, don't you? Then Santa swiftly hopped down from the roof top by sliding down an icicle hanging nearly to the ground, and then he fell DEEP, DEEP into the snow. "My stars it is moving!" Santa began quickly digging and digging inside the mound of snow. Shocked and amazed, he scooped out a shivering white ball of fur.

"Oh! Dear! It is a puppy! How did it get inside the snowball? I cannot leave this puppy here or it will die." He cradled the nearly frozen puppy in his gloves to warm and comfort it. He tenderly hugged the puppy as its soulful tiny eyes peered into Santa's with sadness.

"Little puppy do not be sad. I am taking you home to a magical place of love and great joy, the North Pole." He knew Mrs. Claus loved animals and always wanted a puppy, even though she never told him. Now it was time to make her wish come true. Then Santa whistled, "Hey Rudy! While I slide down the chimney, shine your light on the puppy so it keeps warm." Gently he wrapped it in the sleigh blanket while Rudolph shined his nose on low-beam. The shivering puppy huddled under the blanket and heard singing in the distance, "Buon Natale," Merry Christmas in Italian. The puppy was so exhausted from being buried under the heavy snow that it slipped into a deep, deep sleep.

After placing gifts under the tree, with the blink of an eye Santa zipped up the chimney. He then placed the puppy inside the furry lining of his coat. Santa called out, "Tally HOOOOOOO!" Rudolph, his eight pals, and the sleigh flew into the twinkling starry sky. Soon Mr. Sun would be rising with rapid speed, and so they finished bringing Christmas gifts to children all over the world. Their job was done and happily they headed home to the North Pole.

Chapter 4

Christmas Customs Around The World

Santa loved the many different Christmas customs and traditions around the world. ZOOOOOOOMING along in the sleigh towards home, he thought about the country of Japan and how on Christmas Eve, he places a gift on the children's pillows. On the sunny island of Jamaica, there is a huge colorful parade the day after Christmas with a dance from Africa called Junkanoo. Western Africa, Sierra Leone and much of Gambia celebrate by having masquerade parties, and the whole community is invited to participate. While in Ghana, after the cocoa harvest on the first of December, the people decorate everything for four weeks and enjoy parties with lots of food.

Spain has a special Christmas treat, a delicious, sweet dessert made with honey, egg white, sugar, and toasted almonds served on Christmas Day, yummy. Poland is another country with a special Christmas Eve dinner called Wigilia, which in Latin means to watch. Whatever occurs at the Wigilia meal is a prediction for the coming year.

Santa always looks forward to visiting Ireland as on Christmas Eve, he is left with a plate of minced pies and Guinness ale; it is like a beer. And the people of Finland on Christmas Eve take a sauna bath before Santa arrives, my how relaxing.

Children in China decorate their homes with beautiful paper lanterns. Very similar to some other countries such as the Philippines, they have a Giant Lantern Festival during the Christmas Season. In Goa, India, on Christmas Eve night they string giant, paper lanterns, shaped like stars, between their homes.

So when you walk through the neighborhoods it is as if you have floating stars above you.

The country of Mexico has many Christmas plays based upon Christ's birth. The children dress up as Mary and Joseph, the angels, the shepherds, even some of the barn yard animals, and the Three Wise Men. They also have many family parties and festivities including a piñata which has seven points representing the Seven Deadly Sins. Children are blindfolded and given a bat to swing at it, and when it breaks there are candies for the children.

In many countries, Christmas time is winter but it is the opposite for other places like Brazil, Argentina, Bali, New Zealand and Australia. It is their summer time and they have Christmas picnics on the beach!

Santa thought how special the world would be if we all learned to respect and appreciate our various customs and cultures. He wished people would learn from one another to celebrate the wonderful differences which make Mother Earth a very, very special place to live.

Suddenly Rudolph's red nose beamed up and lit the sky; this was his signal they were ready to start coming in for a landing. This was the most dangerous part of the flight other than taking off. There was no room for error as Rudolph shined and blinked his nose on high beam, and started to go lower and lower with the eight tiny reindeer following his lead. Their legs were moving at lightning speed while Santa firmly held the reins and guided the reindeer and the sleigh. The sacks of toys were all empty and the weight of the sleigh was much lighter. Rudolph then re-calculated and adjusted the sleigh speed just like a pilot does when flying an airplane. Then they slowed waaaaaaaaaaaaaaay down, carefully moving towards the ground. The reindeer could see the snow and the rooftop of the Elves Workshop. Their hooves, starting with Rudolph, one by one by one started touching the ground, while the sleigh skimmed into the soft, fresh snow. Santa squeezed tightly on the reins, and then like MAGIC the sleigh gently stopped! They landed! But this year there was one thing different when landing at the North Pole, a new addition to the family: a little puppy from Alpicella, Italy.

Chapter 5

Returning Home with A Special Gift

Mrs. Claus was anxiously tapping her feet while waiting for Santa. There was a loud knock on her door, Rat-a-tat! Rat-a-tat! It was Melville the Chief Elf and Rat-a-tatter. She opened the door and Melville excitedly said, "They're here!" She ran as fast as her little feet could move, almost floating, as she grabbed Melville's hand, running outside to be with the other elves to greet them. The elves cheered and squealed with great JOY as Santa got out of the sleigh, undid the bells and ribbon bridle on each of his magical reindeer, and patted Rudolph's head for a job well done.

Melville yelled out to everyone, "It's time to CELEBRATE!" The reindeer stomped their hooves as they were looking forward to the special dinner Mrs. Claus had been preparing for days on end, cooking and baking their special treats. Grass with honey, carrots glazed with cinnamon, lollipops with clover sprinkled with ginger and other delicious food. The elves could not wait to put on some music and dance and sing into the wee hours, celebrating Santa's safe return and Christmas Day.

Santa walked towards Mrs. Claus and gave her a big bear hug and a kiss on the cheek. The festivities were in full swing, RING-A-DING-DING. She fluttered with glee knowing her husband was finally home after his trip around the world. He turned to her and said, "I have a very special gift for you." Ever so gently and carefully, he plucked from inside his furry coat her special gift. He handed to her the little white ball of fur.

She could not believe her eyes as she had always dreamed of having a puppy. A puppy she could play with and watch grow into a big, strong, loving dog. Mrs. Claus was a very unselfish person, always thinking and giving to others. She had kept her secret wish for a puppy to herself. She knew her husband had huge responsibilities fulfilling the dreams and wishes on every child's Christmas Wish List. How could she ever bother him with her special wish? Mrs. Claus looked at Santa and said with excitement in her voice, "Oh my! This is the most wonderful gift I have ever received. Thank you my dear, sweet husband." She looked down, tenderly cradling the little unexpected Christmas gift. She was so overwhelmed with emotion she did not even notice the puppy's soft, snowy white hair.

Mrs. Claus wondered what they would name the puppy. Turning to Santa she said, "You were the one who rescued and saved it. What shall we name it?" "Well," Santa replied, "It is not it! It is a BOY! Yes, I will give him a name and it should be from his homeland, Italy." "I agree," said Mrs. Claus. "Perhaps I can make one suggestion. His first name should start with the letter C to go with his last name which starts with C, Claus." "Hmm," Santa thought out loud. "This puppy is strong and he did survive the cold, damp snow that covered him. He is sort of manly with his thick, curly coat of fur. Plus he does have a noble long nose. I've got it!" Smiling with great pride he said, "His name shall be Carlo. Carlo Claus!"

We all know that Santa has special gifts, including a brain that is built like the fastest computer in the entire world. He knows everything we have learned in school such as adding and subtracting faster than a blink of an eye, and answering the most difficult scientific questions of our universe. So with rapid speed the name was given to the puppy. Mrs. Claus kissed his noble nose and Santa rubbed his furry little head. Now it was time to introduce him to everyone at the party.

Santa tapped a crystal glass to get everyone's attention. Immediately the reindeer stopped eating, the elves stopped dancing, and all eyes were upon Santa Claus. "I have an important announcement to make. First of all, I want to thank the elves for making all the toys, a tremendous amount of hard work! And many, many nights you had to stay up round the clock trying to figure out all those electronic and computer gadgets and cell phones requested by the older children with parent's permission. Second, thank you, Rudy, for your leadership of Team Reindeer. Taking the first leap into the sky is always a bit dangerous, but you did it and off we went without a hiccup! Your nose has guided us through many storms and ferociously foggy nights, but once again we have arrived safely home. Third but never last, to my eight magnificent reindeer, you pulled the sleigh effortlessly. All that practice really paid off, especially on those nights this past November when we had some DOOZYS of snowstorms. Simply put, Team Reindeer, you are AWESOME!

Santa turned to Mrs. Claus holding Carlo. "Finally, I have a very special introduction. This is the newest addition to our wonderful North Pole Family, Carlo Claus. I found him in the hills of Northern Italy where it was snowing heavily in a tiny village named Alpicella; hence, the name Carlo for his heritage." Thunderous applause broke out with the clanging hooves of the reindeer, and Rudolph turned his nose onto spotlight mode to shine upon Mrs. Claus and Carlo. The elves were jumping as if they had springs in their feet and were nearly touching the wood beam ceiling of the workshop. Then they all began chanting and cheering his name, "Carlo! Carlo! We love you, Carlo!"

Chapter 6

Carlo's Special Talents

Carlo would not be cradled in Mrs. Claus's arms for very long as he grew as fast as mushrooms after an autumn rain. Within months he became a gawky, long-legged, curly-topped snowy white poodle. At one year old and fully-grown, he was the same size, maybe a bit taller and a whole bunch thinner, than a yearling lamb. Everyone loved the feel of his fur that was different than most dogs. In fact, each day Mrs. Claus would have to brush him or it would get all jumbled up and matted. Then she would take the fur caught in the brush, get out her loom, and turn the fur into fine yarn for knitting. She made scarves for the reindeer, knitted special pointed ear muffs for the elves, and made fluffy, white blankets for their beds.

Besides his gift of fur, Carlo was quite smart. The reindeer thought he knew their Hoof Language as he always wagged his tail exactly the same amount of times the reindeer struck their hooves. For example, two strikes of hooves meant Santa was coming to the barn and three strikes meant Mrs. Claus was looking for Carlo and four meant the best of all, lunch! And the elves believed the same as the reindeer, that Carlo is one smart doggy. Carlo seemed to know their Elf Secret Signals. They would wiggle their ears, blink and wink at different speeds, slow meaning something different than fast motion. Carlo wagged his tail in reply and the elves were convinced he was talking to them!

Every day was play day for Carlo with the reindeer and the elves, but the first order of the day was following Mrs. Claus as she did her chores. He was just like the nursery rhyme, "Mary Had A Little

Lamb." One day she looked at him and said, "I have a nickname for you my dear Carlo, as you remind me of a lamb!" He looked at her and cocked his head as if intently listening to her (he was so smart he probably knew what she was saying). "You are my Lambie-POOH!" He got up on his hind legs and gave her a big slurp on the cheek. Yep! Everyone in the North Pole thought Carlo was pretty darn special.

Carlo looked forward to his evenings with Santa as he fetched snowballs after dinner. Santa would throw the balls of snow over and over and over again and then would say to Carlo, "Daddy Santa is going to beddy-bye." Before you could say banana split with whipped cream and a cherry on top, Carlo leaped upon the bed in between Santa and Mrs. Claus, dreaming of his many adventures to come.

Carlo dreamed of flying like the reindeer pulling the sleigh on Christmas Eve night. He wanted so very much to fly and prance like them in the moonlight of the evening sky. Carlo did all the doggy things so well. He could catch the fastest snowball from Germaine, the fast ball pitcher for the Elf Snowball Team. He could run as fast as most of the reindeer, especially after they had eaten a heavy meal. Every day Carlo played the game of Hide and Seek with Mrs. Claus. He was so smart that by the time she hid, he would sniff the air and immediately find her! Yes, Carlo had many talents except for one, he could not fly.

Chapter 7

Kerplopping Gets Carlo A Job

It was early spring and snow was still covering the ground. Carlo decided he would practice flying as that was the one way he knew he could go with Santa on that special journey. He had to have a job like the reindeer but he was just a dog. He was the only dog in this magical Kingdom, the North Pole.

Carlo looked around and found the highest rooftop which was the Elves Workshop. It was a pointed roof so that the snow would easily slide off. He carefully climbed up as he made doggy tracks in the snow. The elves were busy making toys but once in a while they would hear him hooooooooooowl as he slipped off the roof! It took some practice but finally he could climb the slanted rooftop without falling.

Then the day came as he mustered up the courage to look waaaaaaaaaaaaaaaaaaaaaaay down below to the ground. He shut his eyes, pretended he was a reindeer, and bravely pranced off the roof! KERPLOP! He belly flopped into the drifts of snow and immediately rolled onto his back. He did not want anyone to know what he was doing and so just in case someone saw him on the ground, he pretended as if he was making snow angel-dogs. Carlo continued hours upon hours repeating the same rooftop maneuver with the same outcome: KERPLOP! KERPLOP! KERPLOP! KERKLOP!

Chief Elf Melville knew what Carlo was doing and said nothing. He would come out after Carlo had been Kerplopping for hours, pat him on the head, and ask, "Would you like a cookie? Would you like maybe two sugar cookies?" Melville had a soft spot in his heart for Carlo; he had always wanted a dog and now he secretly had one. Cookies were his way of encouraging Carlo, and without saying a word he wanted him to understand to try, try, and try again! Soon Rudolph knew what Carlo was trying to do, and he felt so sorry for him that he would bring Carlo cookies from Mrs. Claus kitchen, especially M&M cookies. Both Melville and Rudolph would tell Mrs. Claus they were getting cookies for their team mates, but Mrs. Claus knew better. She heard Carlo's Kerplopping, too.

Rudolph called the Team of Reindeer together for a meeting. He and Melville had an idea to help Carlo and his dream of being with them and Santa on Christmas Eve night. After laying out his plan, he asked the other reindeer if they thought it would work. Prancer, Comet, Dasher, Blitzen and the rest of the team liked Rudolph's solution. Donner said, "Rudy, we are all in this together, go and share it with Santa." Then Dancer, Cupid, and Vixen told Rudolph they would hang around outside the Claus home to cheer him on.

Chapter 8

The Plan

Rudolph took his front hoof and gently tapped on the front door. Santa Claus called out, "Come on in Rudy!" Rudolph explained, "We all know Carlo cannot fly but he has been practicing for months. None of us want him to get hurt jumping off of the roof and I have a plan." Santa responded, "Go ahead Rudy, I am all ears and we do need a plan." Rudolph explained "How about letting him come with us Christmas Eve? He can sit next to you on the sleigh, and he can bark, ruff-ruff, woof-woof and howl out Christmas Carols to us. You know how much the Reindeer Team loves carols. It will make the ride even merrier, and a lot more fun." Santa wrinkled his brow, puckered his lips, shook his head from side to side, and finally let Rudolph see the twinkle in his eyes, a good sign! "You know Rudy that might just work. He could be a very fine addition to the team. Let me talk it over with Mrs. Claus and get her opinion, as you know how much she loves her Lambie-POOH!"

Mrs. Claus listened keenly to her husband's solution to Carlo's wanting to fly. She was well aware of his KERPLOPPING as she saw him often pretending to make angels-dogs in the snow. "What do you think of your training him to learn Christmas Carols and you can accompany him, for now, on the piano to learn them? He can sing to us and it will be so much fun to have him with us. Picture him howling Christmas Carols to our friend the midnight Moon! And you know it isn't easy for those eight tiny reindeer and Rudy pulling the sleigh piled high with gifts and me with my expanding waist line from your excellent cooking! Please, dear, say yes?" pleaded Santa.

Mrs. Claus had great wisdom and Santa admired her greatly for it. She explained to him that everyone had a job but Carlo. The elves made the gifts, the reindeer pulled the sleigh, Santa made it all happen, and her job was baking, cooking and caring for them all... especially Santa. Now it was time for Carlo to have his own special job, Chief Christmas Caroler on Christmas Eve. It would really be a wonderful addition to the team as he would woof and ruff and howl his little heart out, hitting the high notes of the carols. She turned to Santa and said softly, "Yes, he can fly with you and the team of reindeer." Mrs. Claus explained to Santa how worried she has been about Carlo jumping off the steep, slanted roof over and over again. She had only one request. "Dear Husband, you know and I know, you have had some very bumpy take offs and landings with some scratches and dents on the sleigh as you ZOOOOOM along from rooftop to rooftop. I want Carlo to have a doggy sleigh belt so he is safe and secure. Carlo does not have your magical powers or the ability to fly; he is a dog, my precious Lambie–POOH!" Santa replied, "Yes, as usual you are absolutely right! I will talk to Melville immediately and have the safest most secure doggy sleigh belt made for him. I promise nothing will ever happen to him, he is our baby." Santa told her she should have the honor of sharing the good news with Carlo.

Mrs. Claus whistled for Carlo, and he ran into the house wagging his tail and then sat at attention. He knew something was up and wondered if his attempts to fly had gotten him into trouble. He thought, "Oh! No! There goes my flying. I have no job and that means no sleigh riding and helping on Christmas Eve." He cast his eyes downward, feeling empty hearted until he heard Mrs. Claus say, "Santa and I have decided you need a job." She explained the plan to him of being the Chief Christmas Caroler on the sleigh. All of a sudden his ears perked up, he cart wheeled across the floor, did back flips over and over, then squealed with glee and jumped into her arms. His wish had come true, and now it was time to practice the carols and learn them by heart so he could perform every year during the Christmas Eve sleigh ride.

From then on, instead of jumping off the roof of the Elves Workshop, Carlo would practice his Christmas Carols while Mrs. Claus played the piano. His Woof! Woof! Woof! sounded superb and his high note of HOWLING was pitch perfect! The reindeer would often sneak over to the doorway and crack it open to listen to him, while the elves who have super-duper hearing hummed along as they made the Christmas toys.

Chapter 9

Carlo Joins the Team

The months flew by lickety-split like a rocket roaring towards the planet Jupiter, and then the big day arrived, Christmas Eve. The elves finished making all the toys, carefully placed them in heavy sacks, and then dragged them onto the sleigh. The reindeer were harnessed with red satin ribbon tied with bells. Rudolph tested his nose for all the different light beams and then turned to Santa and blinked his nose with a special signal, "All systems go!" Santa then turned and kissed Mrs. Claus on the cheek, holding her hand, promising that Carlo would be safe in their evening travels across the twinkling skies.

Mrs. Claus had made a special gift for her Lambie-POOH, a hand knitted sweater in heavy wool to protect him from the cold. She made it into the colors of the Italian flag: green, white and red stripes with a matching knit cap that had his name, Carlo, knitted in green yarn and decorated with shapes of red and white candy canes. She strapped the cap on his head, hugged him and squeezed him ever so tight. Carlo gave her a big slobbery lick upon her cheek and then Santa said, "It's time to fly!" Mrs. Claus stood back away from the sleigh with the other elves while Melville squeezed her hand, worried as always about the takeoff.

WHOOOOOOOOOOOOOOOOOOSH! Rudolph was in the lead with his nose beaming brightly, lighting up the pitch black sky. Behind him the crew of eight tiny reindeer air lifted into the night pulling up! And up! And up! And up! The sleigh was off the ground with Santa Claus, Carlo, and sacks of toys to be delivered to the excited children around the globe. Soon Mrs. Claus, the elves and Melville could no longer see them in the sky, only the blinking of the stars shining brightly upon the fresh, new snow. They headed back, the elves to their workshop and Mrs. Claus to her home. She kept busy baking and cooking while the elves kept busy decorating the workshop for the big party upon the return of Santa and the sleigh.

The elves loved their workshop and their decorations made it so festive and full of lights. Winston, the lighting engineer elf, knew how to string lights from every corner, ceiling and wall. Ginger Snap, why she loved to put garlands of green and white and red streamers from the top of the inside of the roof all the way down to the floor. Lilting Lilla set the tables so there was enough room for the reindeer to sit, as you know they have long legs. She had special short tables for the elves and much higher tables and chairs for the reindeer. Holly and Norton put together the sound system; they had to be very careful as the elves had sensitive ears. They also had to get the music for dancing as everyone knows how much the elves love to boogie-woogie!

All of the elves had two things in common: their love for children and their skills to make them toys. In their workshop could be found tools the likes of which could not be seen anywhere else on Earth. On many occasions they made their tools simply by imagining them. They would think of the tool they needed and BAAAM, it would appear. They thought up tools that could make toys in milliseconds. POOF! The toy was ready to be wrapped. The elves had tools they could command to make things simply by the sound of their voice. The only problem was an elf named Guthrie; he had a very soft voice and sometimes the tool made a doll when it was supposed to be a ball!

Every elf loved to work and every elf was happy knowing they had made a child's Christmas wish come true. Santa would share with the elves his evening adventures of putting gifts under the Christmas trees. For some children it was a mango or a banana tree, and for other children, presents were placed on their pillows. Each country had its traditions and customs. Oh! The elves were full of joy to hear the stories, knowing the gifts they had built were somewhere around the world making a child's Christmas bright and merry.

The elves knew the special meaning of Christmas; it is not what we receive but what we give and this was a lesson the elves knew very well. The elves were very kind and wanted children to be given love and joy so that when they grew up they would do the same for their children, for their families, friends and for strangers.

Chapter 10

Returning to Alpicella

Carlo was singing while reindeer flew high and low depending upon the weather, the peaks of the mountain ranges, the lakes and oceans. They had visited many countries but Carlo had a super surprise for Santa and the reindeer. As they flew over San Francisco, California, Carlo had a special song for them as he Ruffed, Ruffed, Ruffed, "I Left My Heart in San Francisco." He was proud of himself for learning this tune while listening to Mrs. Claus playing it over and over again on the piano. They flew farther southwest over the crystal blue ocean into the Hawaiian Islands. Carlo began to Woof! Woof! Woof! "Mele Kalikimaka," a Hawaiian Christmas song. As the gifts were brought to the different countries he had a tune for each one of them. Arriving in Germany

61

he softly Arff! Arff! Arffed! "Silent Night;" while crossing the border into France he Bow-Wow-Wowed "The First Noel."

Santa had purposely left Italy towards the end of the trip. He didn't know how Carlo would feel about returning to his home. But he knew the time had come to head towards Northern Italy. Delaying just a bit longer, Santa turned the sleigh south from France to the beautiful Italian island of Sicily, the largest island in the Mediterranean Sea. Heading North, they followed the Apennines mountain range from Sicily to the toe of the "boot" of Italy, through the central part of the country until they reached the North, crossing many of the twenty regions of Italy.

The reindeer pranced along in the sky as they drew closer and closer to their destination, Alpicella. Santa gave a tug on the reins and down they glided into Northern Italy. Landing on the rooftop of the home where he found Carlo in the snow. Santa wondered if Carlo would want to stay in Alpicella. Would Carlo want to go looking for his parents? Santa gently patted Carlo's head and off he went. Flinging the sack of toys over his shoulder, he gave one long glance to Carlo, and then slid down the chimney to deliver the gifts.

In the distance Carlo could hear caroling in Italian, "Buon Natale" Merry Christmas. He vaguely remembered hearing this song when he was buried under the snow. He suddenly realized that this must be where he was born. He knew he was home. But was it REALLY home?

Tears sprang into his big brown eyes as he knew deep in his heart that he loved Santa and Mrs. Claus. He then looked around, looked at the deep snow where Santa found him as a puppy and said to himself, "My home is where I am loved and I love them. My home is the North Pole." He understood the greatest gift is not his snowballs, toys, cookies or where he was born. No matter where you come from, even if you are different and cannot fly like a reindeer or hear like an elf, home is your heart surrounded by those you love.

Chapter 11

The Rest of the Story

Carlo waited patiently for Santa and then he heard a cackling sound. What was that? He smelled the crisp winter air and sniffed and sniffed. He knew there was someone nearby, and so he got off the sleigh, put his nose to the ground and followed it over to the chimney. Lo and behold! Facing him, upside down was a witch on a broom with a dog. It was Florinda. She had a friendly face and he looked deep into her green, far away eyes and thought, "Hmm, I bet this is one of those goofy witches Santa is always talking about to Mrs. Claus." She then turned her broom right side up with the dog and said, "My name is Florinda, the witch, I live in Beigua." She looked at his knitted cap, Hey! You have an Italian name, Carlo!

Well, you must be the dog we have been looking for all year long!" Carlo looked at the goofy witch. What was she babbling about?

Florinda said, "Let me explain to you Carlo what happened last Christmas Eve. We were supposed to have a Snowball Bocce Ball Tournament against the Banshees. Esmeralda was to make a magical snowball that when thrown at the Banshees' balls would make their balls disappear. But there was no snow and we needed to make some! Tizianna loves to make potions, and concocted one to cover Beigua with snow. Little did we know it would be the wrong formula, and then the snow started and would not stop! Meanwhile Esmeralda decided to add a stronger spell onto the snowball and right before our eyes, the snowball in her hands started to sprout white hair, four legs, two ears and a tail! It was a puppy! We named it Nevicata, Snowfall. Yes, it is you! We had no idea that the Banshees were hiding behind the trees and watching everything. They were going to get revenge on us for our little plan of trickery that went astray. They wailed so loud they called up the North wind at gale forces and swhoooooooooooooooosh you were blown out of Esmeralda's hands!

You went rolling down into the deep snow like a snowball gathering more and more snow; you slid down the mountainside going towards Alpicella. We panicked because we could not get on top of our brooms to fly since the wind was so mean and forceful. Each time we tried to mount our brooms, the North wind blew and we were thrown off and hurled into the forest while the Banshees wailed and laughed. Eventually we were able to make a potion to stop the snow and bring out the sunshine to melt it. But it was too late. We searched everywhere on the dirt roads, in the bushes, on the tree tops, in the caves, all around the village of Alpicella. We went door to door asking everyone had they seen a little white puppy. The answer was always the same, No! The night you rolled down the hill we sang Christmas carols, hoping you could hear us and be comforted until we could rescue you.

The witches didn't know that Carlo remembered their singing and was comforted when he heard the song, Buon Natale. Florinda went on and on with the story. "We even asked Zorabella to look into her crystal ball to find you. All she saw was snow, but then again she uses a snow globe as her crystal ball! But this morning, she said the dog is coming here and he is with Santa! We aren't so sure of her predictions but we wanted to believe you were safe and sound. So that is why I was sent to find you, Snowfall, Nevicata. Whoops! I mean Carlo."

All this time that Santa was inside delivering presents, he listened to Florinda's story. He then gave a blink of his eyes and up the chimney he flew. The goofy witches of Beigua were all floating in the sky. Santa turned to their fearless leader Luce Lampa. She had her pet rooster, Roberto, sitting onboard the broom; he was cock-a- doodle- dooing! Roberto was supposed to make this sound in the early morning, not at night, but this was a rooster of a Beigua witch! He was as goofy as they were! These witches loved their farm animals just as much as their pet dogs and cats.

Stern but amused, Santa looked over his shoulder and there was Zorabella twittering while on her broom with her pet goat, Frederica, who was munching the straw on the back of the broom! Flying next to Frederica were two other witches Avalina and Tiziana, riding together with a black cat named

Bruno, who had golden eyes, and his pal Romeo, a striped grey and white cat whose eyes lit up crimson red at night. Both cats were rubbing against the broom while meowing together, as if singing to their friends Avalina and Tiziana. Meanwhile, Esmeralda was swishing along on her broom and then stopped in mid-air to put night cream, for wrinkles, on her pet pig named Patrizia.

Yes, these Goofy Witches of Beigua were quite silly and fun loving!

Santa had a twinkle in his eye, as he could barely hold back his laughter. He cleared his throat and then again sternly looked at Luce and said to her, "Luce, promise me that for the next three days neither you or any of your witches will cast any spells or concoct any potions. It was your witches' misguided spells that created the blizzard snowstorm last year that could have frozen the entire village, including the puppy."

Luce lowered her eyes and softly said to Santa, "You have my word and the promise of all the witches of Beigua; we will behave ourselves." Santa told them he would send a corrected version of their book of spells, but they must keep their promise. She then repeated, "We promise on the honor of the Ligures Tribe." Then she and her rooster, Roberto, swooped down to Santa, gave him a pinkie swear, then slapped her forehead like a salute, and again said, "We give you our word."

Carlo was grateful for the wacky wonderful witches' mistake that brought him into this world, even if he was meant to be a snowball! Luce fluttered over to him and asked, "Will you forgive us? We meant no harm." Carlo wagged his tail as fast as he could to let them know all is forgiven. She swooped down and kissed him on his head and whispered, "You will always be our special Nevicata, Snowfall." Then the cackling chorus of Beigua witches screeched out, "We hope to see you again next year, Buon Viaggio, Safe Travels!"

Santa took the reins and said to them, "It's time to clear the skies!" The witches flew off happily cackling and singing, Buon Natale, Merry Christmas. Carlo thought, yes I hope to see them next year, too. He then nuzzled Santa with his noble nose, giving him a gigantic slurp on the cheek. Santa chuckled and patted him on his head, and then from way down in his belly he shook and bellowed, "HO! HO! HO!" With a quick snap of the reins and a jingle of the sleigh bells, they flew into the Italian sky, with Carlo happily howling the song "Santa Claus Is Coming to Town!"

They went into the magical night flying high above the clouds bringing presents to the children as Carlo sang his tunes. The reindeer loved his music, shaking their antlers from side to side, especially when he sang their favorite song "White Christmas."

They merrily glided back to the North Pole, their night's work finished and Mr. Sun beginning to peek over the horizon. Presents all around the world were making children happy, and Carlo was delighted that his first sleigh ride had been so rewarding. But would he get to ride again on Christmas Eve and sing his songs? Just as the sleigh was making its final landing, Carlo began howling and woofing, "Jingle Bells" and they slid to a smooth-silky five-star landing.

Mrs. Claus, Melville and all the elves rushed to the sleigh and then unharnessed the ribbons and bells on the team of reindeer. Santa unbuckled Carlo who then pranced like a reindeer, and when he spotted Mrs. Claus he leaped into her arms. Wagging his tail with great happiness, jumping and skipping into the air, he licked her face as she hugged her precious Lambie-POOH.

Santa turned to Carlo and announced, "You are now officially our Reindeer Dog! You will come with us every Christmas Eve. You have another year of new songs to learn and to practice with Mrs. Claus." Carlo bowed his head towards Santa. He was so proud of his new job and title that he broke out into a woofing song, "We Wish You a Merry Christmas," and everyone joined in singing and clapping for Carlo, the Reindeer Dog.

Mrs. Claus turned to her family: the elves, the reindeer, Santa, and Carlo. "Now it is time to celebrate and have our Christmas Party!" The reindeer were starving from the long evening of flying, and they ran to eat and drink while the elves sang and danced.

Santa and Mrs. Claus sat on the sofa with Carlo's curly, snow white head in Mrs. Claus's lap.

Santa turned and said to her, "I have quite a story to tell you about those goofy witches in Beigua and how Carlo came about." She looked at him, smiled and said, "It will be fun to hear all about them after you get some rest, my dear. I find your stories so hilarious about those goofy witches."

Santa was so happy and grateful to be home as he recalled that freezing night when he found the little white puppy beneath the piles of snow. He had kept his promise to Mrs. Claus and had brought Carlo home safe and sound. Santa looked into Carlo's sweet kind eyes, gave him a big hug and whispered into his ear, "Sometimes we are given a very special unexpected gift and that's the best gift of all, LOVE."

MERRY CHRISTMAS, BUON NATALE

TO YOU!

Love Carlo, the Official Reindeer Dog

Translation and Pronunciation Guide

English	Italian	Phonetic Pronunciation
alpine	alpini	‹al·pì·no›
broom	scopa	‹scó·pa›
cat	gatto	‹gàt·to›
dog	cane	‹cà·ne›
elf	elfo	‹èl·fo›
goofy	sciocco	‹sciòc·co›
grandfather	nonno	‹nòn·no›
grandmother	nonna	‹nòn·na›
magic	magia	‹ma·gì·a›
Merry Christmas	Buon Natale	‹buò·no› ‹na·tà·le›
moon	luna	‹lù·na›
puppy	cucciolo	‹cùc·cio·lo›
reindeer	renna	‹rèn·na›
rooster	giallo	‹giàl·lo›
safe travels	Buon Viaggio	‹buò·no› ‹viàg·gio›
Santa Claus	Babbo Natale	‹bàb·bo› ‹na·tà·le›
sleigh	slitta	‹ṣlìt·ta›
snow	neve	‹né·ve›
snowfall	nevicata	‹ne·vi·cà·ta›
wild boar	cinghiale	‹tʃin'gjale›
witch	strega	‹stré·ga›

Acknowledgments

When I was a little girl, I would walk alongside my Nonno Antonio while he checked the vegetable crops on his farm. He would tell me of stories about growing up in Alpicella, Italy. My Nonno always had a twinkle of merriment in his sky blue eyes. I used to laugh as he shared with me his youthful adventures and I thought, "Alpicella must be a very special place to live." I have discovered this to be true and for that reason have made Alpicella an integral part of both of my books.

When my Nonno Edoardo Bertuccio suddenly passed away at an early age, his wife, my Nonna Maria, moved into our home. When I was five years old, I would sit in our kitchen to watch my Nonna cook and she would tell me stories. I would listen to her intently and tried to imagine what it would have been like. She had an abundance of stories and I never tired of hearing her tell me of Italy and immigrating to America. She was the Regina of Story-telling, the Queen, and her best stories were about stregas, witches. She was from a tiny village, called Pé, and she told me of a strega who roamed her village. My poor Father, Carlo, did not want to hear these stories because they frightened him. My Mother Rosa also declined to listen to her mother's stories. And so it was an audience of one, me! Nonna told me of the dark forests in the hills above Alpicella, of a place called Beigua where there lived stregas and the wild cinghiales, boars. I was captivated.

There is no doubt I have been influenced by my grandparents. I am humbly grateful to be called the granddaughter of four Italian immigrants from the region known as Liguria. It was only through their courage in coming to America that I have been the recipient of the wonderful opportunities our great Nation has to offer. Nonno Antonio Ferro from Alpicella and Nonna Antonietta Rusca Ferro from Stella San Bernardo; Nonno Edoardo Bertuccio from Montesorro and Nonna Maria Vallerga Bertuccio from Pé; I am forever grateful to you. Ti amo, sempre.

Carlo Ferro was my kind, compassionate and loving Father. His favorite holiday was Christmas because he couldn't wait to eat home-made raviolis and cream puffs. He had a special fondness for animals, especially dogs, and ever since he suddenly passed away, I always wanted a Standard Poodle named after my Father. And so it was one day, I brought home my Standard White Poodle and named him Carlo. He is my precious puppy, my Lambie-POOH, whom I love dearly. And it is they, Carlo my wonderful Father and Carlo my four-legged pal, who were my inspirations for writing "The Reindeer Dog."

As Santa has elves, so I have had many helpers in writing this book:

Thayer "the Darer," you would not stop pestering me, nor allow me to slough off so that I would write to my fullest potential. You were a task master that dared me to bring out my very best.

Linda "Lightning" Berry, you have been a golden treasure whom I love as a sister. You are the Empress of words, punctuation, sentence structure and spelling. You have done this twice for me with two books; it is beyond measure. You are the best.

Miss Alyssa Rose, Ginger Snap, you listened patiently as I read my story to you from the very first draft. You are my special elf, sharing your vision of the illustrations for this book.

Andrew the Messenger, you were so quick in delivering my manuscripts to the North Pole for review. You calmly helped me, even during the times when I thought I would pull out my hair.

Thank you, my special helpers.

Printed in the United States
By Bookmasters